THE DARKEST HOUR

ISSRILLA
THE CREEPING
MENACE

With special thanks to Tabitha Jones

For Isobel and Alex

www.beastquest.co.uk

ORCHARD BOOKS
338 Euston Road, London NW1 3BH
Orchard Books Australia
Level 17/207 Kent St, Sydney, NSW 2000

A Paperback Original
First published in Great Britain in 2013

Beast Quest is a registered trademark of Beast Quest Limited
Series created by Beast Quest Limited, London

Text © Beast Quest Limited 2013
Inside illustrations by Pulsar Estudio (Beehive Illustration)
Cover by Steve Sims © Orchard Books 2013

A CIP catalogue record for this book is available from
the British Library.

ISBN 978 1 40832 398 4

3 5 7 9 10 8 6 4

Printed in Great Britain by CPI Group (UK) Ltd, Croydon, CR0 4YY

The paper and board used in this paperback are natural recyclable
products made from wood grown in sustainable forests. The
manufacturing processes conform to the environmental regulations of
the country of origin.

Orchard Books is a division of Hachette Children's Books,
an Hachette UK company

www.hachette.co.uk

ISSRILLA
THE CREEPING
MENACE

BY ADAM BLADE

ORCHARD

Dear Reader,

My hand shakes as I write. You find us in our hour of greatest peril.

My master Aduro has been snatched away. The kingdom is on its knees. Not one, but two enemies circle our shores – Kensa, the banished witch, has returned from Henkrall. With her stalks Sanpao, the Pirate King. Strange magic is afoot, stirring not just in Avantia but all the kingdoms, and I sense new Beasts lurking.

Only Tom and Elenna stand in the way of certain destruction. Can they withstand the awful test that will surely come? This time, courage alone may have to be enough.

Yours, in direst straits,

Daltec the apprentice

PROLOGUE

Rokk the Walking Mountain stared into the mist that covered the peaks of Tion. There was evil in the mist, he could feel it. The red sun glanced over the rocky horizon. Rokk shifted his limbs to catch its rays, growling in pain as his stone joints crunched and grated. He was so tired. He longed to hibernate, to allow his body to break apart and become one with the land. But he couldn't sleep, not while...

Rokk tensed, clenching his fists.

The land groaned as stone was forced against stone. Here it was again – the sickness that was destroying his mountains. Anything that hurt Gwildor, hurt Rokk, and he almost cried out with the pain of it. The tremor passed. The Beast sighed and trudged through the deserted valley.

As the sun rose higher, a barren plain opened up before him. It was scattered with rocks and skeletons, and was wreathed with mist. *Here is the source of this wickedness*, Rokk thought.

A flicker of movement caught Rokk's eye. He turned his head but found nothing other than pale, broken skeletons. As he took a great stride forwards, a shadow fell across him from above. Rokk swivelled his head towards the sky. What he saw

made his core churn.

A curved, wooden vessel hovered overhead. It was driven by canvas sails that billowed in the wind. *A ship*, Rokk thought, *but surely ships are things of water. They don't sail on air!* His body rumbled as he recognised a Beast's skull on its flag. Something was very wrong.

Suddenly, his attention was drawn downwards. He could feel a crawling sensation, up his leg...

One of the skeletons was clinging to him. It was about the size of a horse, but shaped more like a lizard, with dead black holes for eyes.

The dead can't move, Rokk thought.

The creature didn't feel like bone either, it felt more like...slime. As the thing moved again, its outline glimmered. Rokk could see that the lizard did have flesh, but the flesh was as clear as water. *What evil is this?* he wondered.

Boom! Rokk stamped, trying to shake the slithering thing away. The earth trembled, but still he could feel the sticky feet scurrying across the back of his knee.

He craned his neck to see it and glimpsed a barbed tail, flickering through the air.

Rokk roared as pain blossomed in his leg. The creature had stung him! And now it was on his knee. Anger welled inside him like an erupting volcano. He lifted his fist, mustering all his strength...then swung it towards the thing.

The creature moved, and Rokk's fist smashed into his own leg. His knee buckled and the ground rushed up to meet him.

Rokk tried to turn as he fell, to crush the lizard-Beast, but the creature was too fast. Rokk heard a terrible, slithery hiss as it flitted across his body. He landed with a bone-shaking crash.

He realised he'd been tricked. Without him to look after it, the kingdom was in peril. The creature climbed onto his chest, the glistening point of its tail lifted for another deadly strike.

The tail snapped towards Rokk's stony heart.

Then, nothing...

CHAPTER ONE

A FRIEND IN NEED

Tom tossed and turned under his blankets. *I should try to rest*, he thought, *at least until Freya returns with breakfast.* With four more Beasts to conquer, who knew when the next chance for sleep would come? He shifted onto his side. It was no use! He glanced at Elenna, curled up in a blanket nearby. At least she wasn't having trouble sleeping. Tom sprang to his feet, grabbed his sword and slung his shield across his shoulders.

Quietly, he moved away from their sleeping place and trudged towards the tree-line of the Rainbow Jungle. Tendrils of mist curled around him and smothered the jewel-like colours of the plants with ghostly grey. Water dripped from the foliage and the trees rustled with life.

A terrible wail cut through the air.

What was that? Tom quickened his pace. *A scream? Someone's in trouble!*

Another cry set his heart hammering. The sound seemed closer now.

Wet leaves and branches snagged at his clothes as he pushed into the jungle. *Whatever it is must be through here...*

Parting the thick foliage, Tom peered into a clearing.

"Aduro!"

The Good Wizard lay on a stone slab, his face slack and grey. Thick chains ran from his wrists and ankles and disappeared into the shadows. As Tom started forwards in horror, purple lightning seared through the air and slammed into Aduro's body. Tom staggered back in pain. Aduro screamed again as more blasts of magic crackled from every side. The Wizard's back arched and his limbs shook. Tom

fell to his knees, clutching his head.

It's as if I'm feeling Aduro's pain, he realised.

He stumbled to his feet, still half-blind from the purple lightning. He could just make out dark shapes in the shadows – hooded men in long black cloaks. With a shock, Tom recognised the sorcerers from the Circle of Magic. He'd last encountered them at the start of this Quest, when they'd sentenced Aduro to imprisonment. The Good Wizard had helped Tom use the Lightning Path to get to the kingdom of Henkrall, which had angered the Circle.

But what are they doing here, now?

Tom braced himself as the cloaked men raised their hands to unleash another blast. *This can't be real! Aduro's supposed to be in Avantia...*

Tom ran forwards, burning with rage.

"Tom?" Elenna's voice pulled him back. "What are you doing out here on your own?" her hair was still messy from sleep, and her eyes were full of worry.

Tom turned slowly back to the jungle. There was nothing but trees in the mist.

I was seeing things! he realised. *It wasn't real.*

"Tom, you look terrible." Elenna said. "Were you sleepwalking?"

"Not exactly." Tom gave a shuddering sigh. "I saw a vision of Aduro. It was awful. The Circle had him tied up. They were torturing him..."

"But that doesn't make sense," said Elenna. "They were supposed to give us time to put things right. Who could have sent the vision?"

"It couldn't be anyone from the Circle." Tom replied. "They need us to finish this mission. If we don't recapture those Beasts then Kensa wins. Chaos will rule forever and the Circle will be finished."

"Let's go back to camp," said Elenna.

"Maybe Kensa sent it?" Tom said, as he walked beside her.

"Maybe," his friend replied. "With the three kingdoms drawn so close together and ravaged by Beasts, she grows stronger every day. She'd love it if we turned back."

When Kensa had escaped from Henkrall on the Lightning Path, her evil magic had set free six Evil Beasts into the world. It had also forced Avantia, Gwildor and Kayonia dangerously close together. Now these Evil Beasts could attack three

Kingdoms at once!

"But what if the vision's true?" Tom said. "Shouldn't we go back to Avantia? How can we abandon Aduro?"

"Innocent people will suffer if we turn aside from our Quest," Elenna said. "Aduro wouldn't want that."

Silver bounded up to them as they arrived back at the camp. Elenna bent to bury her face in her wolf-hound's fur.

Tom stood by, his thoughts churning. What was the right choice? Whatever he did, it felt as though lives could be lost.

A soft warmth tickled his cheek. Storm, Tom's stallion, had come up behind him. He pressed his forehead against his horse's neck. "I'm so glad you're here with me."

"Tom! Elenna!"

Tom looked up to see Freya walking towards them with a basket of fruit in her hand. His mother had joined them on their Quest when they'd arrived in the kingdom of Gwildor. Now her armour shone like burning gold in the pale morning light, but her face was drawn.

"Here, eat," she said, laying the basket on the grass. "Then we must get going.'

"What's wrong?" Elenna asked.

Freya bowed her head. "Rokk," she sighed. "He's in trouble. I feel his distress even now. I must go to him. It is my duty as Mistress of Beasts."

Tom laid a hand on his mother's shoulder, forcing his tiredness away. Elenna stretched and rubbed her face with her hands, then grabbed two plums from the basket.

"Let's go," she said, throwing a plum to Tom.

Tom caught the fruit and let Storm eat it from his hand. He leapt onto his stallion's back. Now that his mind was made up, he felt alive with purpose. He had to continue his Quest, for the sake of the people of Gwildor. He'd saved the kingdom once, and he wouldn't let Evil Beasts ruin it now. Their Quest lay to the north, among the mountains of Tion where Rokk dwelled.

While there's blood in my veins, I will help him.

CHAPTER TWO

DANGER AHOY!

Tom drew Storm to a halt and swung himself from his stallion's back. Freya landed lightly beside him. She'd been parted from her own horse on the edge of the Rainbow Jungle. *She'll never get over the loss*, Tom thought, his heart squeezing tight.

"Thank you friend," she said, stroking Storm's mane. "But the ground here is rough. We'll walk."

They had ridden hard all morning
and now the mountains of Tion rose
darkly through the mist on either
side.

"What a bleak place!" Elenna said,
looking over the craggy landscape.

"These mountains were once
beautiful," Freya said. "I hope they
will be again."

They toiled up the rocky path in
silence, saving their breath for the
climb. Eventually, they rounded a
bend, and a wide valley opened up
before them. The valley floor was
the same dusty red as the cliffs that
flanked the road. In the distance they
could see the ruins of rock huts: the
village of Tion. Or what was left of it.

Tom glanced at Freya, wondering
if she remembered the last time they
were here. Back then, she had been

under an evil spell and had tried to kill him. But now his mother seemed lost in other thoughts.

"We shouldn't be here yet," she said, shaking her head. "There should still be miles to travel. If the kingdoms keep closing in on each other, soon there will be nothing left of Gwildor."

As Tom followed her gaze he felt a nagging feeling at the back of his mind.

"This place," he said. "There's something about it..."

"I know what you mean," Elenna said. "It gives me the creeps. I'm not surprised the villagers never moved back."

"Death Ledge used to be here," Freya said. "This part of Tion has long been a source of fear."

Death Ledge. Tom thought of his

terrifying climb on his Quest to find Freya's magic gloves... That was it!

"I recognise it now! This is the place where we lost your golden cask, Mother – the one that held your spider-web gloves."

"That's right!" Elenna said. "We'd never have managed to free Rokk without them. Their climbing power saved your life."

"The cask must still be among the ruins," Tom said. "Perhaps we can find it now."

Tom led them towards a pile of rubble overshadowed by what was once Death Ledge. They started to sort through the debris.

Rocks chinked together as Tom shifted them, sending up puffs of dust. Something glinting in the dust caught his eye.

"Mother, here!" he called. "I think
we've found it."

Freya hurried over and lifted the
golden casket. She ran her fingers
across its base. An image appeared,
showing two suits of shining armour.
Tom felt a pang as the first suit
reminded him of his father, Taladon,
the previous Master of Beasts. The
other suit was smaller and set with

jewels. It belonged to his mother.

"I thought this was lost forever," Freya said.

"GHAH-HA-HA!" A guttural laugh rang through the valley.

Tom spun around, his nerves thrumming. It was a sound he knew only too well. *Pirates!*

He crept out from the shadow of the overhang and looked up. Sanpao's flying ship hovered above the next peak. Tom beckoned for the others to join him.

"So Rokk was warning us," Elenna said.

"Maybe," Freya said. "But in that case, where is the Walking Mountain?" Her frown deepened. "I really hope he's all right."

"So do I," said Elenna. "But Sanpao will be here to strip the goldmines,

and Kensa will be close behind.
We have to stop them."

"Yes," said Tom. "They escaped far
too easily back in the jungle." An
image flashed through his mind of
Amictus's precious egg, smashed to
pieces. "Sanpao and Kensa have done
enough damage," he growled. "It's
time they were stopped. We need
to get up to that ship."

"I have to wait for Rokk," Freya
said. "I'll stay here with Storm and
Silver."

"Good plan," Tom said. He laid
a hand on Storm's nose. "You stay
with Mother," he said. "We'll be back
soon."

Elenna put her hand out to Silver.
Her wolf licked her fingers, then went
to sit with Storm. Tom and Elenna
started to pick their way towards

the mountain's base.

"Oh, Tom!" Elenna gasped, pointing at a huge rock, lying off to one side. It looked like a giant fist. "Is that...?"

"No!" Freya rushed past them. "Rokk's hand!" she cried. Her face was grim. "It's been ripped from his arm. Whoever did this must be stopped."

"Then there's no time to lose," Tom said.

Tom and Elenna hurried across the dusty ground and into the shadow of the mountain. Tom looked up at the craggy, red stone trying to pick out a route.

"This is going to be tough," he said.

"Well, we'd better get started then." Elenna hopped lightly onto the cliff-face.

Tom tucked the leather bag that

held his lightning tokens and ruby jewel into his tunic, then reached up and grabbed a ledge next to her. The rock was dusty and smooth and it was hard to find a good grip, but they climbed steadily until Tom's arms burned.

Finally they reached the summit. Tom pulled himself up after Elenna and shook his muscles to get rid of the cramp. They crept to the far side of the narrow ledge and lay on their bellies to look over the edge. Sanpao's ship hovered below.

"Where are all the pirates?" Elenna asked.

Tom scanned the bare decks of the ship. "Up to no good, I'll bet." he said. "I think we should take a closer look."

"And maybe do some damage?" Elenna said.

"Exactly!" Tom said.

They scrambled back from the ledge to stand side by side.

"Ready to jump?" Tom asked.

Elenna nodded. They both sprang forward and raced towards the edge. Tom brought one foot down hard and pushed...

A giddying span of air opened up before him, then gravity clutched

at his stomach as he started to fall towards the ship. Tom braced himself for the impact, then thudded onto the deck. Elenna landed beside him, as softly as a cat. But not softly enough...

"Who goes there?" a gruff voice cried from below. Elenna winced. Then came the sound of heavy footsteps. Tom grabbed Elenna's arm and pulled her behind a crate just as a pirate's shaven head emerged from a hatch in the deck.

CHAPTER THREE

SABOTAGE!

Tom and Elenna huddled behind the crate and looked around the side. The pirate's forearms bulged as he pulled himself through the hatch.

"Nothing 'ere" the pirate bellowed. "Musta been a bird or something."

Tom let out a breath of relief as the pirate retreated below deck.

"Phew! I thought the ship was deserted," Elenna whispered. "We'd better go carefully."

Tom nodded. "Sanpao must be about here somewhere and he'll sniff us out in no time. We'll have to hurry."

Tom slipped down onto his belly and Elenna did the same. Elbow to elbow, they crawled across the deck. There had to be something they could do... Smash a hole in the hull maybe, or rip the sails... No – the pirates would be sure to hear.

"Do you think we could get down to the gun deck without raising the alarm?" Tom whispered. "With no weapons Sanpao won't be nearly as bold."

"If we're quiet," Elenna said. "What will we do when we get there?"

Tom thought for a moment. "Get rid of their gunpowder or disarm their cannon."

"Good thinking," said Elenna.

They stole to the side of the ship and crept towards the stern. Then Tom spotted what he was looking for. A hatch. He pulled its iron handle, raising the door a crack. Voices floated up from below, along with harsh laughter, but Tom couldn't make out what they were saying. Carefully, he opened the hatch the rest of the way then leaned down into the hole.

It was gloomy and hot inside, and smelled of gunpowder and sweat, but at least he could hear what the pirates were saying.

"Hah! My two pair beats your flush. Hand 'em over, Valtek."

"Bad luck, Valtek."

"Shut yer trap if ya know what's good for ya."

"Yeah, yeah. All hot air, you are!"

It sounded like a game of cards, but Tom couldn't see the players. He spotted another crate near the hatch. He raised his head, then turned and lowered himself feet first through the hatch and onto the rope-ladder below. Elenna followed him down onto the gun deck where they slipped behind the huge coil of rope and peered over the top.

Four pirates were sitting around a barrel, using it as a table for their game. Tom studied them carefully. They were all easily twice his size. Knives and whips hung from their belts. Tom scanned the deck, looking for the powder. There were bulging leather pouches strewn about the floor, gunpowder spilling from some. Tom frowned. *They're asking for trouble, leaving powder lying around!*

Just one little spark and...BANG!

Elenna cocked her head towards the pouches and raised an eyebrow. Tom nodded. They crawled side by side across the deck, ducking behind barrels and keeping low so as not to be seen. The boards felt rough and grimy under Tom's hands. He scooped up a powder pouch and tucked it into his tunic. Elenna did the same. They crept onwards, collecting more as they went, keeping well clear of the noisy card game.

Tom packed the pouches into his shirt, reaching for another, then another. *They'll never be able to attack now!*

"Royal flush! And that makes these beauties mine!" Tom heard the chink of coins. He reached for the next pouch.

Clunk! Tom turned sharply to see Elenna holding her elbow, her face twisted in a grimace of pain. It looked like she'd hit her elbow on a crate.

"What was that?" a pirate grunted.

"Frightened of rats now, are yer?" came the response.

"Nah, he's trying to distract us, coz he don't want to lose the round," another pirate said. Tom felt a wash of relief.

"You filthy rotten liar!" There was the sound of a chair scraping across the deck.

Tom slithered behind a crate and took a glimpse at the pirate's game. He could see a pile of powder-pouches near one of the pirate's chairs. The pirates were glaring at each other over the table, almost nose to nose. *Now is as good a time as any...*

Tom crept towards the pouches, keeping as low as he could.

"No one calls me a liar!" one of the pirates shouted as Tom crawled across the floor. He was almost there. He reached – *Yes!* – and grabbed a handful of pouches and drew them towards him.

Tom shrank back as a chair scraped

across the spot where his hand had just been.

"So what yer gonna do about it?" a deep voice growled, then another chair was flung back.

"I'm going to teach yer some manners!"

Tom scrambled away clutching the powder. Time to get out of here quick! He glanced behind him. Elenna was already at the ladder.

The barrel crashed to the ground and heavy feet hit the deck. Tom took his chance. He sprinted for the ladder and climbed up after Elenna, stuffing the pouches into his tunic and drawing his sword as he went.

He pushed his head and shoulders through the hatch out into daylight, then froze. Elenna was being held by a burly pirate, and nearby on the floor lay her pouches, surrounded by at least five other pairs of boots. Tom raised his eyes slowly.

A tattooed pirate held Elenna across his chest, a knife pressed against her throat. Other men crowded behind him, cutlasses at the ready.

Tom felt his face grow hot.

"Well, well, well," a rough voice growled. "If it isn't Master Tom!"

CHAPTER FOUR

FLYING TERROR

"Tom," Elenna spoke through gritted teeth. "I'd be very grateful if you could get me out of this. I don't know how much longer I can stand the stench."

Tom choked back a laugh. Elenna's head was very near the pirate's armpit.

A huge man stepped forward and Tom's smile turned to a scowl as cold anger washed through him. It was Kimal, Sanpao's First Mate.

"So, you've come to pay us a visit, eh?" Kimal said as Tom climbed onto the deck. "Well, we're always glad to receive such great enemies of the Makai." He tipped his head towards Elenna, "The girl is especially welcome." Kimal pressed the point of his knife to a puckered arrow scar on his shoulder, drawing a bead of blood. "I have a souvenir to remind me of our last encounter." He licked his blade, then spat. "Drop your sword, boy!"

Tom did as he was told, then grabbed his shield and flung it through the air. It smacked Kimal across the shins.

"Ow! You little...!" The pirate's face turned scarlet and he hopped about,

clutching his leg. Elenna took her chance. She lifted her feet and swung them back right into the pirate behind her.

Kimal dropped his knife and let Elenna fall to the deck. He doubled up, gasping for breath. Elenna spun and her fist flew again Another man doubled over, his face creased with pain. Elenna's foot whipped out and caught Tom's shield and it whizzed across the deck towards him. He bent to catch it, grabbed his sword and flew into action beside her. They streaked across the ship and leapt onto the poop deck. Tom held his sword ready as the pirates charged towards him. He swung for the nearest pirate, then the next, but he couldn't fight them all.

"There are too many," he cried "We'll just have to keep moving!"

Elenna raised her eyes towards the complicated rigging. Tom grinned, tucked his sword in his belt, then stepped back. He lunged off the poop deck, over the pirate's heads and grabbed the ropes. Elenna jumped up beside him. Tom glanced over his

shoulder. The pirates were almost
at their heels. He hauled himself up
the rigging then climbed hand-over-
hand across it. When he reached the
edge, he spotted something he could
use. He grabbed hold of two thick
rope halyards and handed one back
to Elenna. *Now, if we can just reach the
front of the ship...* Tom pushed off with
his feet and flew.

The wind whipped at Tom as

he and Elenna sailed through the air together. They soared over the shouting pirates towards the tall forecastle.

"Whoa!" Tom let go, bent his knees and dropped onto the deck with Elenna. He looked behind him. The pirates were heading after them and they only had moments to spare. Tom dashed to the gunwale and pulled pouch after pouch from his tunic. He and Elenna tossed them over the side.

Tom allowed himself a flicker of a smile as the last pouch burst on the rocks below. *That should slow Sanpao down.* But then Tom felt his smile fade. They were such a long way up! How would they ever get off? He turned to find the pirates fanning across the deck, blocking their way.

A huge man stepped in front of him,

his teeth bared in a snarl. Tom ran straight towards him then slid down onto his side, skidding through the man's legs. He jumped to his feet...

Tom slammed straight into a fist that felt like a wall. Pain exploded behind his eyes. He staggered and fell to his knees.

When his eyes came back into focus, he saw Sanpao's evil smile. The Pirate King stood over him, arms crossed on his chest. He reached forwards and Tom felt a vice-like grip close painfully around his jaw. His eyes watered as he was wrenched to his feet then off the deck. He dangled in the pirate's grasp.

"I've been waiting for this moment," Sanpao growled. "It's high time you sampled a traditional pirate punishment."

He let Tom fall to his feet, and
Kimal wrenched his arms behind
his back then forced him across the
deck. Tom's shoulders burned and his
breath came in furious gasps of pain.
He glanced across at Elenna, writhing
between two huge pirates. Anger

boiled in Tom's belly.

Sanpao strutted before them, a smirk on his scarred face. *He's really enjoying this*, Tom thought.

"I'm a generous man. So I'll give you a choice," the pirate said. "You can either walk the plank, or there's a keel-hauling if you prefer. We'll drag you right along the ship's belly. Either way, it's a lovely day for it, although the mist rather spoils the view. Take your time. I'm in no hurry."

Two different ways to die. Both horrible.

Not much of a choice...

CHAPTER FIVE

FALLING...

"I want to walk the plank!" Elenna blurted.

"Ha!" Sanpao laughed. "No one's ever wanted to walk the plank." He looked Tom and Elenna up and down with something like respect. "Still. I never will understand you two. You act first, think later. You'd have made good pirates. I almost wish I didn't have to kill you..."

"As if we'd want to be like you!"
Tom shouted. "Second-in-command
to a witch like Kensa? No thanks!"

Sanpao's face turned red and he
bared his teeth, "I don't play second
to anyone! We're partners. Until we
choose otherwise."

"Oh?" Tom looked about the deck.
"Where's Kensa now, then?" Sanpao
glared at him, and Tom sensed his
chance.

"I suppose she's got something
more important to do. Something
that she can't trust to the likes of you.
It's good of you to wait here for her,
ready at her beck and call."

Sanpao thumped the cabin wall
behind him then turned to Kimal.
"Throw these brats overboard before
their whining gives me a headache!"
He turned on his heel and stormed

away across the deck.

Kimal hauled Tom towards the side of the ship and Elenna cried out as her captors yanked her along at Tom's side.

"What are you playing at?" Tom hissed at Elenna. "Why do you want to walk the plank?"

Elenna grinned. "Trust me," she whispered back.

Tom's thoughts churned as the plank got closer. Elenna looked so sure of herself, but Tom could only see one way of getting off this ship, and that was straight down. *Has Elenna forgotten we don't have Arcta's feather?* he wondered. *We can't survive a fall like that!*

He felt a shove from behind and stumbled onto the plank. He glanced down as Elenna stepped up behind

him. The grey mist and broken cloud showed glimpses of jagged rock far below them. He swallowed. *There has to be some way out of this...*

His friend put a shoulder to his back and nudged him along the plank.

"Elenna?" he whispered as he edged forward. "Why are you doing this? You're going to get us killed!"

Elenna looked surprised. "Have you forgotten?" she said.

Tom stared at her. "Forgotten what? My eagle feather doesn't work remember. My powers are all gone!"

"Tom," Elenna said, shaking her head, "I expected you to be way ahead of me on this." Then, before he could act, she raced past him and leaped off the plank.

"Don't!" He watched in horror as his friend fell out of sight, plummeting through the clouds.

"Off you go!" Tom felt the plank being pushed up and down. His stomach lurched as he staggered. His foot landed on thin air.

No! Air rushed passed him and

his insides flipped.

Everything went white as he plunged into an icy cloud...then he was almost blinded as he plummeted back into clear air before hitting the swirling mist. The wind whipped at his sodden clothes.

Tom looked down. Jagged rocks and dusty earth raced towards him.

"Tom!" Elenna called.

Where is she? he thought. Then something touched Tom's back and his teeth rattled as he was pulled upwards with a jolt. He looked round. *Elenna!*

"You can fly? But...?"

"Not quite," she laughed and nodded over her shoulder. A pair of leather wings was strapped across her back.

"The Henkrall wings!" Tom cried.

He hung in her arms, dizzy with relief. They'd been given the wings on their last Quest in the mysterious kingdom of Henkrall.

"Well, I had a feeling we might need them again," Elenna said. "I've worn them under my tunic for so long it took me a while to remember I had them."

"Argh!"

Tom and Elenna looked up at the furious cry from above. Sanpao was scowling over the gunwale.

"Unbelievable!" he raged. "You, filthy, rotten..." The Pirate King shook his fist at them.

Tom laughed as he and Elenna swooped away, then banked gently towards the ground. Tom spotted Storm below. And there was Freya, waving. Beside her, Silver turned in happy circles.

Elenna slowed and lowered them to the ground in front of their friends.

"Perfect landing!" Tom said.

Silver bounded over and sniffed at the wings, then licked Elenna's face. "It's alright, I'm fine," Elenna said, ruffling the wolf's ears.

"How did it go?" Freya joined them.

"Let's just say that's the last time I walk the plank," Tom frowned.

"Oh? I thought it was fun," Elenna said, grinning.

Tom started to laugh, but then he saw the expression on Freya's face. She looked almost sick with worry, and he felt a flush of guilt.

She must sense something, Tom thought. He pulled out his ruby jewel. It glowed softly, and Tom felt a strange tremor of panic run through him. "Rokk's in danger," he said, stroking Storm's mane. "Let's go."

They picked their way together through the rocks and boulders.

"We'll reach Bone Valley soon," Freya told them as they walked.

"Bone Valley?" Elenna looked up. "That doesn't sound good."

"It was just a barren valley once," said Freya, "but so many animals have died there, caught in storms off the mountains, that now it's a giant graveyard. It's a dangerous place, full of sorrow."

"Danger and sorrow." Elenna frowned. "That sounds like just where an Evil Beast would hide."

"Then that's where we need to be," Tom said. He scowled into the mist. "And there's no time to lose. All three kingdoms are at stake."

CHAPTER SIX

BONE VALLEY

"I don't like it either, boy," Tom said as
Storm snorted and tossed his head. He
rested a hand on his horse's flank and
peered into the mist. Ghostly shapes
swirled and broke apart, revealing
thousands of bones glimmering in the
silvery light. Bone Valley. Tom fought
back a shiver. Storm's hooves scuffed
at the stony ground as the others
arrived beside them.

Silver growled softly in his throat.

"It's all right, Silver," Elenna said. "They're just old bones."

"No," Freya said. "They're more than that. They're graves. And they mustn't be disturbed. The poor souls that perished here must be left in peace, otherwise they could rise again. The whole kingdom would be in danger."

Tom and Elenna guided their

animals into the greyness ahead.

The sound of their footsteps was deadened by the mist – it hemmed them in so that Tom felt trapped. Storm shied and whickered as shadows shifted around them.

"Easy, boy!" Tom said, and gently pulled him onwards.

In places the fog was so dense that Tom couldn't see his feet. Then it would swirl away, revealing more bones in its sickly light. Tom shifted his shoulders to shake off a creeping unease. This fog wasn't natural – it had all the marks of a Beastly presence.

"Oh!" Elenna exclaimed.

Tom followed her gaze. A massive curved bone lay at her feet. She crouched and Tom bent beside her. The bone was very smooth, and it was hollow.

He felt a thrill as he ran his fingers

across its surface. "It doesn't look like a normal bone," he said. "It looks more like a claw. But the creature must have been huge!"

Freya bent her head beside Tom's. "I can't believe it..." she whispered. "This must have belonged to Cycron the One-Eyed Tiger. He was the Seventh Beast of Gwildor, but he was lost...oh, long ago. Before my grandmother's time. I'd begun to think he was a legend."

"We have a lost Seventh Beast in Avantia too," Tom said. "Spiros the Ghost Phoenix. This must be another way our lands are twinned."

"Look!" Elenna had moved away from the group. "There are craters all over here. And this rock has been smashed by something huge!" She ran her finger along a crack in a boulder. "There must have been a terrible

Battle of Beasts here once. Maybe that's what killed Cycron?"

"No," Freya bent to study a scorch mark on the ground. "These marks are new," she said. "There must... Oh!" Freya gasped.

Tom felt a rumble in his chest and the ground beneath him shook. He planted his feet wide as the shaking became stronger. Small rocks skittered down the valley walls and pattered to earth.

Elenna grabbed Tom's sleeve as a shadow fell across them. She pointed at a huge, dark shape projected onto the mist. The shadow loomed taller and taller, until finally the mist parted and a figure walked towards them. It was a giant man of stone. *Rokk*. Tom breathed a sigh of relief. *Thank goodness he's safe*.

But then Rokk's eyes met his, and

Tom felt a chill run through him. There was no friendship there, just a cold, angry stare. Rokk's right hand was missing leaving a jagged stump. He lumbered towards them, his limbs flailing wildly. Then he opened his mouth and roared.

The sound made the valley shudder and shook Tom to his bones.

"Rokk! Stop!" Freya cried, but Rokk continued rampaging towards them.

"I'll try to reach out to him with the jewel," Tom shouted.

He felt in his leather bag and his fingers closed over the smooth, cool ruby. Instantly his mind was filled with a sense of Rokk's great fury.

Rokk! Tom cried out with his mind. *It's me, Tom. I'm here with Freya – the Mistress of Beasts.*

But Rokk stumbled onwards,

crushing boulders under his feet.

We're here to help! Tom told him.

He staggered as a horrible, slithery

hissing filled his mind. What was it?
It was so angry and full of hate. Then
a name came to him from Rokk – it
sounded like a Beast's name.

Issrilla.

A picture formed in Tom's mind of
a giant skeleton lizard. Its flesh was
transparent and its barbed tail lashed
from side to side as the lizard gazed
from empty sockets.

I control Rokk now! the image hissed.
His body's mine! The Beast laughed, and
the sound scraped across Tom's nerves.

Rokk straightened clumsily, then
swung back his huge left arm...

Tom turned to his friends. "Run!
Now!" he shouted. "Rokk's out of
control!" Storm and Silver sprang
away like lightning, and Freya and
Elenna ran for the cover of nearby
rocks. Tom darted behind a column

of stone just as Rokk brought his fist down against the cliff-face.

Tom slammed his hands over his ears and threw himself to the ground. The earth shook under him and the clatter of falling rocks filled the air. Tom staggered to his feet and peered from behind the column. Rokk was swinging his massive head from side to side, searching for prey. Except it wasn't Rokk. It was the Evil Beast that controlled him. Tom stepped out from behind his cover and met Rokk's cavernous eyes.

"While there's blood in my veins, I will free you!" he shouted.

But to free Rokk, we'll have to fight him.

They had no choice. They'd have to gamble with Rokk's life, and hope that they could win.

CHAPTER SEVEN

FIGHTING BLIND

Rokk towered above Tom. Their eyes locked together. Issrilla's hissing cry crept through Tom's mind like venom, but he held his ground.

"Tom!" Freya shouted. "Rokk's heading towards the bonefield! We can't risk him crushing the bones!"

I have to lead Rokk away from here! Tom squared his shoulders. He lifted his sword and shield. "Come and get me!" he cried.

Rokk lurched towards him. Tom's heart hammered but still he didn't move. *Come on... Just a bit closer...* Tom waited. *Now!*

Just as the shadow of Rokk's foot fell across him, Tom turned and bolted away from the boneyard. Thick clouds of fog billowed across his path and he could hardly see a thing. A rush of wind hit him and he skidded to a stop. Something huge was swooping close... He turned to run but a wall of fingers slammed down, blocking his escape. His stomach lurched as Rokk's great fist closed about him and swept him into the sky.

The hand opened and Tom staggered to his feet. He found himself staring straight into the empty darkness of Rokk's hollow eyes. He saw a flicker

of movement and shivered with
revulsion. Rokk's eyes weren't empty
at all! There was something slithering
about inside. Something made of
bone and glistening jellylike flesh.

Issrilla is inside the Good Beast! Tom
realised. *That's how she's controlling
him!*

The Evil Beast hissed with laughter
then made a sound like a geyser
blowing. Before Tom had a chance to
wonder what it meant, Rokk's hand

swooped upwards and Tom's breath was torn away as he was tossed into the air.

His stomach flipped as he turned over and over in the mist.

The air was knocked from his body as he hit the earth. Every part of him stung as he scrambled to his feet. He glanced about, but all he could see was fog. If only it would clear!

A shadow flitted across him. *What was that?* Tom listened, as he climbed to his feet. He could hear Rokk raging and stamping nearby but there was another, quieter sound. The crunch of gravel under feet... Tom drew his sword from its sheath.

Something grabbed his shoulder and Tom swung around, ready to strike...

"Tom! It's me," Elenna said.

"Elenna!" Tom lowered his sword in relief. "The Beast's inside Rokk's eye. It's sending him out of his mind."

"Inside Rokk?" Elenna frowned. She ducked as a great boulder crashed down somewhere nearby.

"It's some sort of creeping, skeleton lizard covered in slime," Tom said. The earth trembled. "We need to get her out of there, or Rokk will smash this place to pieces."

"Poor Rokk!" Elenna said. She thought for a moment. "Maybe we can climb him? We managed the cliff all right."

"The cliff wasn't trying to kill us," Tom said.

They ran side by side towards the thunder of smashing rocks. Through a gap in the mist Tom glimpsed one of Rokk's pillar-like legs. He hurtled towards it and leapt.

Tom slammed against cold stone, and clung on with his hands and feet. Elenna landed beside him. He pulled himself higher but then a shadow swooped above him, blocking out the light. *Rokk's fist! If that connects, he'll crush us flat!*

"Elenna! Run!" Tom and his friend threw themselves clear just in time.

Rokk's fist smashed right through his own leg. Tom ducked and covered his head as lumps of stone whizzed past him.

As the air cleared, Tom looked up to see Rokk tottering, his broken leg and arm flailing as he tried to catch his balance. A strangled, fearful hiss shuddered through the air.

"Issrilla!" Tom muttered. "She's afraid."

Rokk's broken leg hit the ground like a mighty oak being felled. The Beast staggered, then straightened and somehow caught his balance. Rokk seized his fallen leg and slammed it back into its proper place with a grinding sound. Issrilla's hiss grew to a rattling cry, but Tom smiled grimly. The sight of Rokk's fallen limb had given him an idea. *Issrilla needs Rokk in one piece*, he realised. *If I can convince Rokk to break apart, Issrilla will be forced into the open!*

Tom grabbed his ruby jewel, and at once Issrilla's terrible hissing anger filled his senses. He gritted his teeth and forced his mind to clear, then sent an image pulsing out. It was of Rokk's severed hand.

Issrilla tried to drown out his thoughts with a loud hiss. Tom focussed harder, feeling Issrilla somehow pushing him back. Sweat streamed down his face and his muscles shook with the effort. His energy was draining away...

Tom drew on all his remaining strength. He made one last mighty thrust with his mind...

Yes! He felt a flicker of the Rokk he knew. A low rumbling voice echoed in his mind. *Hibernate?* Rokk said, his voice confused.

Yes, Tom replied. *Fall apart…*

Tom's body sagged with exhaustion. A deep vibration in the land told him Rokk was carrying out their plan. The slow tremor built to a wild juddering as Rokk started to thrash about. Tom staggered as a boulder crashed to the ground nearby. The Good Beast was crumbling apart. Massive rocks the

size of buildings crashed through the
air. Dust billowed and the ground
trembled. Tom hugged himself close
to the ground.

Finally, the sound of falling rocks
turned to a trickle of stones and sand.
Tom clambered to his feet, coughing.
A mound of gravel beside him shifted,
sneezed, and unfolded into a familiar
figure.

"Elenna!" Tom cried. "Are you all right?" His friend took a shaky breath, and brushed some gravel from her hair.

"Just about," she said. Then something moved at the edge of Tom's vision. Something that almost matched the land. Uncoiled, the Beast seemed impossibly huge. Issrilla! She had escaped Rokk's broken body and now she was on the loose. Tom darted after the ghostly shape, but Issrilla was already lost in the mists of Bone Valley. Frustration welled inside him.

"She'll be almost invisible in there!" he cried.

"Then we'll hunt the Beast inside Bone Valley,' Elenna said.

"But we can't disturb the bones," Tom reminded her. "If we do, the

whole kingdom could be in danger."
Tom shifted the shield on his
shoulder. "Are you with me?"

Elenna unhooked her bow from her
shoulder and brought it round to hold
in her fist. "Always," she told him.

CHAPTER EIGHT

HIDE AND SEEK

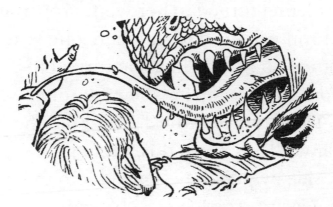

Tom gave a piercing whistle. Storm's answering whinny reached him a moment later.

Silver arrived first, slipping his nose silently under Elenna's hand. Storm and Freya followed behind him.

As Tom explained what had happened, Freya's face darkened.

"Beast preying on Beast!" she said, shaking her head angrily. "We have to make Kensa pay for this."

"But first we must defeat Issrilla," Tom said.

Elenna turned to her wolf. "You and Storm will need to stay here one last time," she said. Then she turned to Tom. "I'm ready for some hunting."

Tom drew his sword. Freya did the same. "Let's finish this," Tom said.

Side by side they stepped into the boneyard. The fog was thickening all the time, drifting in uneven banks. "Let's split up," Tom said. "We'll never find Issrilla like this. Call if you find her. Otherwise, we'll meet back here."

The three of them parted and headed in different directions, their weapons at the ready.

Tom trod softly through the bones, listening as he went. Soon he could no longer hear the footsteps of his friends, but he could feel something else in the mist. A sinister vibration. The hair on his neck stood up, and he turned around. The mist swirled, but there was nothing...

"*Hsssss!*" The sound came from behind him. Tom spun around, but saw only mist and rocks. His thumping heart slowed. *She's playing with me!* He shook away his frustration and stole onwards through the fog, his sword raised and his shield in front of his breast.

A stone dropped to the ground nearby. Tom froze. He could hear the slither of something moving. He glared about him, but he couldn't see a thing...

"*Hsssss...*"

There was the sound again, like the

sigh of shifting sand.

Something lashed across Tom's
shield and drops of burning slime
splattered his arm. He tried to flick
the stuff away, but it was boring into
his flesh. His eyes watered and he
gasped for breath. He scraped at the
venom with his sword, and gulped
in air. The burning sensation at last
faded, and he looked in horror at his
arm. Holes pitted his flesh.

"*Hssss, hsss, hsss!*" Issrilla's sickening laugh brought Tom back to his senses, but he couldn't see the Beast anywhere. He flexed his burning forearm. *Where is she? How can I fight her if I can't see her?*

The fog before him thinned as the sun finally broke through the clouds. Tom scanned the bonefield. He ran his eyes quickly over skeleton after skeleton, looking for a lizard's form.

There! Something shimmered. Tom's eyes snapped back to the spot. Issrilla lay curled on top of a pile of bones, her flesh rippling in the pale light. She cowered as the sun's rays struck her body, then started to worm her way into the bones. They clacked together as her head and back disappeared into the mound. Her tail flicked, and Tom gasped as he saw

some of her transparent flesh pucker
and shrivel in the sun. *So you do have
a weakness*, he thought. *Sunlight!*

And he'd seen something else as
well. A glint of turquoise from deep
within her body. Was that blue-green
bone the source of her power?

Issrilla darted away. But Tom
felt a surge of hope. *This Beast isn't
invincible…*

He peered into the mist. The bones
lay thick on the ground this deep into

the heart of the bonefield. A clear path of disturbed debris curved away from him where Issrilla had passed. *I can follow her trail!*

"Tom! Where are you?" he heard Elenna's distant cry. But he couldn't stop now. The fog grew thicker the further he went, brushing his skin like cold fingers. He breathed hard and was sweating, but still felt chilled to the bone. He was a long way from the others, but if he could just lure Issrilla into the light...

A lithe tail of bones flickered through the air in front of him. He jumped, but too late.

It hit him across the shins. Tom tripped and put out his hands to shield his face, then rolled over the ground, skidding to a halt just a hand's breadth from a deadly curved bone. Tom thought he recognised it, but a hiss made him spin around.

He came face to face with Issrilla's empty stare. The Beast stood tense, as still as ice, watching him and waiting. Tom's fingers tightened about the hilt of his sword. He held her gaze... then swung. His sword sliced through the mist, lashing for Issrilla's face. She almost seemed to smile as his blade parted the air above her. Then, as

quick as a darting snake, she
was gone.

Tom heard her vile laugh as she
slithered away.

"Come back here!" he cried. He
pounded the hilt of his sword against
the ground in frustration. Then his
eyes rested on the smooth curved
bone again. Of course! An image of
Cycron came to Tom's mind – a giant
tiger-Beast with a fierce, glowing eye,
swiping the air with a huge paw.

Yes! Tom thought. *That's what I need
– the help of a Beast to fight a Beast.* He
looked into the mist and clenched his
fist. *Issrilla, I'm coming for you!*

CHAPTER NINE

A VILE FOE

To move the bones was to risk the
kingdom. But without Cycron's
help, the kingdom would be ruined
anyway. Tom had to take this last
chance. He sheathed his sword.
"Forgive me, friend," he said, "but
I need your help." He lifted the claw,
which was lighter than it looked, and
curved to a deadly point. He tucked
it under his arm then crept to the

edge of the boneyard.

He quickened his pace as he saw his friends' shadows through the mist.

"Tom!" Elenna cried. "Did you find Issrilla?"

Tom held out his shield arm. The burns scattered across his flesh oozed with pale fluid. "You could say so," he growled. "She has some sort of burning venom."

Elenna's face paled. "Are you all right?"

"I don't think it's poisoned," Tom said, ignoring the doubt that fluttered in his stomach. Even as he said the words, he could feel something travelling up his arm from the bite wound. "Look," he showed Elenna Cycron's claw. "I think we can defeat Issrilla with this." They hurried to join the others.

"Tom! What have you done?" Freya cried, rushing towards him. "Cycron's claw – you shouldn't—"

"Cycron will understand," Tom said. "He was sworn to defend this land. His spirit is with us now, I'm sure of it."

Freya rested her hand on the claw and closed her eyes for a moment. Then she sighed and met Tom's eyes. "You're right. Cycron will help us if he can. But how?"

"I know Issrilla's weakness," Tom said. "Sunlight sears her flesh, and I think her strength comes from a glowing turquoise bone. If we can get to that..." Tom met Freya's eyes, then Elenna's. "I need something to distract her," he said. "Do you still have the energy to run?"

Elenna nodded.

Freya drew her sword. "I'll run to the ends of the kingdom and back if it will help defeat evil," she said.

"Let's go," Elenna cried. They dashed into the bonefield, springing over bones and rocks as they ran.

Tom followed at a distance. His eyes swept back and forth from one side of the valley to the other, straining to spot any hint of movement. All he could see through the mist were the hollow eyes of the dead skulls staring back at him...

Something shimmered among the pale, mist-wreathed bones. Another skeleton with dead eyes, but this one moved. *Issrilla!* She was creeping through the debris, her glistening belly low to the ground. But she was ignoring Elenna and Freya and heading straight for Tom!

She whipped forwards like a snake, her tongue flickering. Tom gasped and sprang back. Issrilla reared to strike and Tom brought up his sword.

"She's here!" he cried, bringing the flat of his blade against Issrilla's bony snout. The Beast span away, tail flicking angrily. Tom stood with his sword raised, ready for the next

attack. He swallowed. Elenna and Freya were running towards him.

Issrilla watched him with flat black eyes, then lunged straight for his face. Tom leapt back and to the side and sliced the mist with his sword. Venom splattered against the claw as Issrilla twisted and shrank from his blade. Tom stepped back, his heart thundering, and sent Cycron's mighty claw spinning towards Freya. His mother snatched the claw from the air. Then, in one fluid movement, she dived forward, rolled and slammed the claw deep into Issrilla's tail.

The Beast gave a scream like ice breaking and flailed from side to side. Her tail was pinned to the ground. Tom raised his sword above his head, his eyes on Issrilla's turquoise bone. With a horrible bubbling sound, the base of the Beast's tail dissolved away. Issrilla gave a hiss of rage and darted into the mist. Tom stared in dismay at the rest of Issrilla's tail, still pinned to the ground like rotten meat on a butcher's block.

No! Tom gritted his teeth. Why hadn't he thought about this before? Issrilla was a giant lizard, and lizards could detach their tails. How could he hope to beat such a vile opponent with just his human cunning? No super-speed. No strength. He couldn't even send his shadow away to deceive her. He was...

Something hit his legs and lashed around his boots. Issrilla's tongue! She stared at him through vacant eyes, then tugged.

Tom landed on his side. He felt a searing pain in his ankle as venom seeped through his boot. She'd struck again.

"Get off me!" he cried

One of Elenna's arrows buried itself in the tongue, and Issrilla's released him with a hiss of pain. In the blink of an eye, she'd flitted away. Tom scraped frantically at the slime on his boots. He winced. As well as the burn on his ankle, something sharp was digging into his side. Of course! Tom felt a surge of hope and fumbled in his tunic. He wasn't without powers!

"She went that way!" said Elenna, running up to his side and pointing.

Tom stood gingerly and put an arm out to stop his friend. "I need to face her alone," he said.

Elenna nodded, but frowned uncertainly.

"Trust me," said Tom.

His fingers closed around his ruby and he sent out his thoughts to this Beast.

Instantly, Tom was buffeted by Issrilla's vile thoughts. He could feel her watching him. He pulled the ruby from his tunic, along with his bag of coloured lightning tokens. He rummaged inside. Red lightning? No. Purple? He set that aside. As he took hold of the gold token he felt a crackle charge across his skin. That was the one.

Tom sheathed his sword. *This is all or nothing!* He staggered across the bonefield, scanning the ground as he moved, pretending to look for Issrilla. But he didn't need to see her. He could hear her thoughts.

Come to Issrilla, foolish boy... Just like your wicked father...all tricks and treachery...

The grating of Issrilla's thoughts grew stronger and stronger as Tom picked his way through the bones. He could feel the tingle of her excitement prickling all over his body.

One more step, my little...

Tom whipped back his arm as Issrilla reared up. Then he threw the lightning token. Time slowed as the gold disk whizzed through the air...

The token plunged into jelly-flesh and struck Issrilla's glowing bone. The Beast's skeleton glowed as brightly as a lightning flash, forcing Tom to shield his eyes.

Issrilla let out a scream. As Tom looked again he saw her flop to the ground. Her flesh steamed and boiled then trickled from her bones. A choking vapour rose from the Beast's body, making his eyes sting. Tom

watched, transfixed as her skeleton
stiffened for a moment, then clattered
to the ground and lay amid the
puddle of melted slime.

Tom shuddered. Gwildor was free
of the creeping menace at last.

CHAPTER TEN

DANGER ON EVERY SIDE

"Great shot, Tom!" Elenna cried.

"1 couldn't have done it without you two," said Tom.

"We should scatter those wide apart," Freya gestured to the pile, "so there's no way she can come back."

Tom nodded, rubbing his burnt arm. "And there's someonc else to thank too."

He touched his ruby and felt a low

rumble run through him. He grinned. It wasn't the rumble of an earthquake. It was a deep, contented snore.

"Rokk's hibernating," he said.

A blinding light dazzled him. Tom squinted into the brightness and saw a shape flickering. It was no more than a shadow, and it disappeared, but it was a shape that filled him with dread – Kensa! Tom's sword sliced the air but hit nothing.

Elenna spun around with her bow, trying to find a mark. Freya wielded Cycron's claw like a scythe.

"Ha!" It was Kensa's evil laugh.

Tom hurled himself towards the cackle. At the same time he heard a strangled cry from behind him, followed by a thud. Tom turned, terrified at what he might find, just as the light vanished, leaving behind a veil of smoke.

As the smoke cleared, Tom looked around for his friends. He saw a huddled shape on the ground and icy fingers clutched his heart. It was Elenna, bent over Freya's crumpled body. Tom rushed back to his mother's side.

"I'm all right," Freya said weakly, "but... No!"

"What is it?" asked Elenna.

"Cycron's claw!" said Freya. "I let Kensa take it from me!"

Tom helped his mother up. "It's not your fault," he said. "Kensa is cunning."

Elenna put a hand out to each of

them. "Come on. Let's get out of this graveyard. Silver and Storm will be frantic with worry by now."

Tom trudged behind Elenna. Freya walked beside him, head bowed in thought. Tom felt as miserable as she looked. He'd succeeded in another Quest, so why did he feel so unhappy? He couldn't guess what Kensa wanted with Cycron's claw, but it definitely wouldn't be good...

"Daltec!" Elenna sprang forward. Tom looked up to see a familiar figure waiting with Silver and Storm. Daltec stepped towards them, his brow creased with worry.

"Elenna! Tom!" he said. His voice sounded hoarse with exhaustion. "I trust you were successful on your Quest?"

"Issrilla is defeated," Tom said.

"Gwildor is free."

"Well done!" Daltec grinned. "And with the Mistress of Beasts at your side," Daltec took Freya's hand and bowed low, "how could you fail?"

Freya smiled and shook her head.

"It's good to see you," Tom said. "But surely you haven't come all this way to congratulate us."

"Alas, no." Daltec's face fell. "I have grave news."

Despite Daltec's worried look, Tom almost smiled. His young friend was definitely starting to sound more like a wizard.

"Thanks to Kensa's magic, Kayonia now lies to the north," Daltec said, "and it is ravaged by terrible Beasts." He looked dismayed. "Everything's in chaos. People are suffering."

Tom put his hand on Daltec's shoulder. "Don't worry," he said. "If we ride hard

we can be there in a few days."

"Too long!" Daltec shook his head.
"No. I will have to use my magic..."

"But Daltec," Elenna cried, "the
Circle will strip you of your powers
if they find out."

"Lives are in danger," Daltec said.
"It's a chance I'll have to take. What
use is magic otherwise?"

"You're right," Tom said. "We're ready when you are."

"I must bid you goodbye," Freya smiled and nodded at Elenna, then stepped forward and took Tom's hand. "My duty is here, in Gwildor. Good luck in your Quest, my son," she said. Freya held Tom's gaze for a moment, her eyes full of emotion. Tom thought she would say something more, but finally she dropped his hand. She started off through the mist, turning once to wave before she vanished out of sight.

Tom stared after her, his thoughts in turmoil. So many lives depended on his actions. He thought of Aduro, still held captive. And now Daltec would face prison too if he was caught. And all they were trying to do was to keep their people safe!

While there's blood in my veins, Tom vowed, *I will not fail them.*

Join Tom on the next stage
of the Beast Quest when he meets

VIGRASH
THE CLAWED
EAGLE

Win an exclusive
Beast Quest T-shirt and goody bag!

In every Beast Quest book the Beast Quest logo is
hidden in one of the pictures. Find the logos in books
67 to 72 and make a note of which pages they appear
on. Write the six page numbers on a postcard and
send it in to us.
Each month we will draw one winner to receive
a Beast Quest T-shirt and goody bag.

THE BEAST QUEST COMPETITION:
THE DARKEST HOUR
Orchard Books
338 Euston Road, London NW1 3BH
Australian readers should email:
childrens.books@hachette.com.au

New Zealand readers should write to:
Beast Quest Competition
4 Whetu Place, Mairangi Bay, Auckland, NZ
or email: childrensbooks@hachette.co.nz

Only one entry per child.
Final draw: JANUARY 2014

You can also enter this competition
via the Beast Quest website: www.beastquest.co.uk

Join the Quest,
Join the Tribe

www.beastquest.co.uk

Have you checked out the Beast Quest website?
It's the place to go for games, downloads, activities,
sneak previews and lots of fun!

You can read all about your favourite Beasts,
download free screensavers and desktop wallpapers
for your computer, and even challenge your friends
to a Beast Tournament.

Sign up to the newsletter at www.beastquest.co.uk
to receive exclusive extra content and the
opportunity to enter special members-only
competitions. We'll send you up-to-date info on all
the Beast Quest books, including the next exciting
series which features six brand-new Beasts!

Get 30% off all Beast Quest Books at www.beastquest.co.uk
Enter the code BEAST at the checkout.

All books priced at £4.99.
Special bumper editions priced at £5.99.

Orchard Books are available from all good bookshops, or can
be ordered from our website: www.orchardbooks.co.uk,
or telephone 01235 827702, or fax 01235 8227703.

FREE COLLECTOR CARDS INSIDE!

Series 12: THE DARKEST HOUR
COLLECT THEM ALL!

Three lands are in terrible danger from six new Beasts. Tom must ride to the rescue!

978 1 40832 396 0

978 1 40832 397 7

978 1 40832 398 4

978 1 40832 399 1

978 1 40832 400 4

978 1 40832 401 1

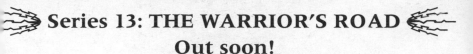

Series 13: THE WARRIOR'S ROAD
Out soon!

Meet six terrifying new Beasts!

Skuric the Forest Demon
Targro the Arctic Menace
Slivka the Cold-hearted Curse
Linka the Sky Conqueror
Vermok the Spiteful Scavenger
Koba the Ghoul of the Shadows

SPECIAL
BUMPER
EDITION!

**Watch out for the next
Special Bumper
Edition
OUT JUNE 2013!**

Join Tom on his Beast Quests
and take part in a terrifying adventure
where YOU call the shots!

NEW ADAM BLADE SERIES

Coming soon 2013

Robobeasts battle in this deep sea cyber adventure.

Read on for an exclusive extract of
CEPHALOX THE CYBERSQUID!

THE MERRYN TOUCH

The water was up to Max's knees and still rising. Soon it would reach his waist. Then his chest. Then his face.

I'm going to die down here, he thought.

He hammered on the dome with all his strength, but the plexiglass held firm.

Then he saw something pale looming through the dark water outside the submersible. A long, silvery spike. It must be the squid creature, with one of its weird robotic attachments. Any second now it would smash the glass and finish him off...

There was a crash. The sub rocked. The silver spike thrust through the broken plexiglass. More water surged in. Then the spike withdrew and the water poured in faster. Max forced his way against the torrent to the opening. If he could just squeeze through the gap...

The jet of water pushed him back. He took one last deep breath, and then the water was over his head.

He clamped his mouth shut, struggling forwards, feeling the pressure on his lungs build.

Something gripped his arms, but it wasn't the squid's tentacle – it was a pair of hands, pulling him through the hole. The broken plexiglass scraped his sides and then he was through.

The monster was nowhere to be seen. In the dim underwater light, he made out the face of his rescuer. It was the Merryn girl, and next to her was a large silver swordfish.

She smiled at him.

Max couldn't smile back. He'd been saved from a metal coffin, only to swap it for a watery one. The pressure of the ocean squeezed him on every side. His lungs felt as though they were bursting.

He thrashed his limbs, rising upwards. He looked to where he thought the surface was, but saw nothing, only endless water. His cheeks puffed with the effort to hold in air. He let some of it out slowly, but it only made him want to breathe in more.

He knew he had no chance. He was too deep, he'd never make it to the surface in time. Soon he'd no longer be able to hold his breath. The water would swirl into his lungs and he'd die here, at the bottom of the sea. *Just like my mother*, he thought.

The Merryn girl rose up beside him, reached out and put her hands on his neck. Warmth seemed to flow from her fingers. Then the warmth turned to pain. What was happening? It got worse and worse, until Max felt as if his throat was being ripped open. Was she trying to kill him?

———

He struggled in panic, trying to push her off. His mouth opened and water rushed in.

That was it. He was going to die.

Then he realised something – the water was cool and sweet. He sucked it down into his lungs. Nothing had ever tasted so good.

He was breathing underwater!

He put his hands to his neck and found two soft, gill-like openings where the Merryn girl had touched him. His eyes widened in astonishment.

The girl smiled.

Other strange things were happening. Max found he could see more clearly. The water seemed lighter and thinner. He made out the shapes of underwater plants, rock formations and shoals of fish in the distance, which had been invisible before. And he didn't feel as if the ocean was crushing him any more.

Is this what it's like to be a Merryn? he wondered.

"I'm Lia," said the girl. "And this is Spike." She patted the swordfish on the back and it nuzzled against her.

"Hi, I'm Max." He clapped his hand to his mouth in shock. He was speaking the same strange language of sighs and whistles he'd heard the girl use when he first met her – but now it made sense, as if he was born to speak it.

"What have you done to me?" he said.

"Saved your life," said Lia. "You're welcome, by the way."

"Oh – don't think I'm not grateful – I am. But – you've turned me into a Merryn?"

The girl laughed. "Not exactly, but I've given you some Merryn powers. You can breathe underwater, speak our language, and your senses are much stronger. Come on – we need to get away from here. The Cyber Squid may come back."

In one graceful movement she slipped onto Spike's back. Max clambered on behind her.

"Hold tight," Lia said. "Spike – let's go!"

Max put his arms around the Merryn's waist. He was jerked backwards as the swordfish shot off through the water, but he managed to hold on.

They raced above underwater forests of gently waving fronds, and hills and valleys of rock. Max saw giant crabs scuttling over the seabed. Undersea creatures loomed up – jellyfish, an octopus, a school of dolphins – but Spike nimbly swerved round them.

"Where are we going?" Max asked.

"You'll see," Lia said over her shoulder.

"I need to find my dad," Max said. The crazy things that had happened in the last few moments had driven his father from his mind. Now it all came flooding back. Was his dad gone for good? "We have to do something! That monster's got my dad – and my dogbot too!"

"It's not the Cyber Squid who wants your father. It's the Professor who's *controlling* the Cyber Squid. I tried to warn you back at the city – but you wouldn't listen."

"I didn't understand you then!"

"You Breathers don't try to understand – that's your whole problem!"

"I'm trying now. What is that monster? And who is the Professor?"

"I'll explain everything when we arrive."

"Arrive where?"

The seabed suddenly fell away. A steep valley sloped down, leading way, way deeper than the ocean ridge Aquora was built on. The swordfish dived. The water grew darker.

Far below, Max saw a faint yellow glimmer. As he watched it grew bigger and brighter, until it became a vast undersea city of golden-glinting rock rushing up towards them. There were towers, spires, domes, bridges, courtyards, squares, gardens. A city as big as Aquora, and far more beautiful, at the bottom of the sea.

Max gasped in amazement. The water was
dark, but the city emitted a glow of its own
– a warm phosphorescent light that spilled
from the many windows. The rock sparkled.

———

Orange, pink and scarlet corals and seashells decorated the walls in intricate patterns.

"This is – amazing!" he said.

Lia turned round and smiled at him. "It's my home," she said. "Sumara!"

Calling all Adam Blade fans!
We need YOU!

Are you a huge fan of Beast Quest? Is Adam Blade your favourite author? Do you want to know more about his new series, Sea Quest, before anybody else IN THE WORLD?

We're looking for 100 of the most loyal Adam Blade fans to become Sea Quest Cadets.

So how do I become a Sea Quest Cadet?

Simply go to **www.seaquestbooks.co.uk** and fill in the form.

What do I get if I become a Sea Quest Cadet?

You will be one of a limited number of people to receive exclusive Sea Quest merchandise.

What do I have to do as a Sea Quest Cadet?
Take part in Sea Quest activities with your friends!

ENROL TODAY!
SEA QUEST NEEDS YOU!

31901055839957